JUV
LARRY
H.I.
Frozen

DRAWN

Go on all of Zac's missions in

ZAC POWER

24 HOURS TO SAVE THE WORLD ... AND GET HOME FOR DINNER

FROZEN FEAR

BY *H. I. LARRY*

ILLUSTRATIONS BY *ASH OSWALD*

SQUARE FISH

FEIWEL AND FRIENDS
New York

With special thanks to the spies of
Years 2 and 3 (2005) of the St. Michael's unit of GIB
for their top secret mission support.

SQUARE
FISH
An Imprint of Macmillan

Library of Congress Cataloging-in-Publication Data
Larry, H. I.
Frozen fear / by H. I. Larry ; illustrations by Ash Oswald.
p.   cm.   — (Zac Power)
Summary: A spy for the Government Investigation Bureau, twelve-year-old Zac is sent to Great Icy
Pole to learn why planes are suddenly making frequent flights over a remote a research station.
ISBN 978-0-312-34656-0
[1. Spies—Fiction. 2. Sabotage—Fiction. 3. Adventure and adventurers—Fiction.]
I. Oswald, Ash, ill. II. Title.
PZ7.L323783Fro 2008   [Fic]—dc22   2008035013

Originally published in Australia by Hardie Grant Egmont
Published in the United States by Feiwel and Friends
First Square Fish Edition: May 2012
Square Fish logo designed by Filomena Tuosto
Illustration and design by Ash Oswald
mackids.com

10 9 8 7 6 5 4

AR: 4.4 / LEXILE: 640L

CHAPTER...
...ONE

First rule of surfing? Never, ever drop in. If you're about to ride an awesome wave but someone gets in the way and takes the wave instead, it's called dropping in.

Zac Power had read all about it in his favorite surf magazine, *Pipelines*.

Things had been dropping in on Zac way too much recently. Zac wanted to surf along all day as though life were one big wave. But school, his parents, his brother Leon, and most of all, his job as a top secret spy for the Government Investigation Bureau (or GIB for short), kept dropping in and getting in his way.

Not this time, thought Zac. It was summer vacation and the Power family was driving down to their beach house at Point Relaxation. The whole family might work for GIB, but even spies need vacations.

Zac's surfboard was strapped to the roof rack. His electric guitar was in the trunk. He was going to play all night. Loudly.

Zac switched his SpyPad to game mode. Should he play *Grudge Match 3* or *Total Chaos* first? It didn't matter. He had loads of time to play both. He wouldn't be needing his SpyPad for missions!

On missions, Zac used his SpyPad as a computer, mobile satellite telephone, laser, and code-breaker—you name it!

Beside him, Leon was playing games on his SpyPad, too. Not the cool ones though. He was playing *Rockin' Calculus*.

Leon worked for GIB as well, but as a home-based Technical Support Officer and Official Gadget Expert.

In the driver's seat, Zac's dad made a

left turn. "Low on gas," he said. "Better stop here."

They pulled into a gas station. It was full of cars towing boats and trailers. Everyone seemed to be going down to the beach.

Zac's dad whistled when he saw the price of gas.

"It's those gasoline tankers mysteriously sinking," Zac's dad said to his mom. "It's created a shortage, which has driven the price of gas sky high."

Zac's mom nodded in agreement. She pulled her purse out of her official GIB handbag—which came with a laser-guided penknife disguised as a lipstick and Total

Knockout Tissues. These special tissues are injected with a chemical that makes you fall asleep on the spot when you blow your nose with them.

Zac shrugged. He knew it was bad that gas was so expensive. But really, what could *he* do about it?

Zac hopped out of the car to stretch his legs.

Suddenly, there was a sound of thunder overhead. Air swirled around the gas station, picking up dust and candy wrappers. It was strange, because the sky was a perfect blue. But the thunder was getting louder.

Zac shivered. It felt like the sun had

gone away. Zac didn't know it, but a huge black shadow was creeping over him.

Leon, watching from the car, dropped his SpyPad.

"Zac!" he yelled. "Get out of the way!"

But with the car windows rolled up, Zac couldn't hear him.

Then . . .

THUNK!

Suddenly, something thumped Zac hard on the back.

In the next second, Zac was lifting off the ground! Something was pulling him upward!

The wind got stronger. The thunder got louder. Zac's hair blew all over the

place. Underneath him, people scattered,
screaming. He was 50 feet off the ground
and still rising fast.

Zac looked up. He was hooked by the
back of his T-shirt onto a cable. And the
cable was dangling out of a helicopter!

A man appeared at the door of the
helicopter. He shouted into a megaphone.

"Zac Power!"

Zac squirmed in midair. If this person knew his name, it must be an enemy agent trying to kidnap him. Zac had to get free!

"This is Special Secret Agent Fox, Airborne Division."

Zac was level with the helicopter door now. Special Secret Agent Fox took hold of Zac and dragged him into the helicopter.

Zac puffed and panted on the helicopter floor. Fox read from a memo.

"This is an official message from GIB."

GIB! Well, in that case, thought Zac, *enemy agents aren't kidnapping me. Things might be OK.*

Fox coughed importantly and read on.

"We wish to inform you that your

summer vacation has been cancelled, starting now."

In that case, things are definitely not OK! Zac had been looking forward to summer vacation for a long time.

"Got a sweater, Zac?" Fox was saying. "It'll be cold on this mission."

"Why? Where is it?" asked Zac, angrily.

"The Great Icy Pole. Know anything about it?"

"No," said Zac, feeling very grumpy.

And he didn't want to, either.

CHAPTER... ...TWO

In a matter of minutes, the gas station and Zac's family were just a speck in the distance. And so was his summer vacation.

"Here," Fox said, handing him a disc. "Your mission."

With a deep sigh, Zac loaded the disc into his SpyPad.

...loading...

CLASSIFIED

MISSION RECEIVED 2:54 PM

Suspicious activity has been recorded in the Great Icy Pole. Our surveillance tells us that lots of extra planes and boats have been coming and going, seemingly with no good reason.

YOUR MISSION
- Go to the Great Icy Pole.
- Investigate suspicious activity.
- Report back to GIB Mission Control within 24 hours.

END

VACATION MODE
>>> OFF

Zac's shoulders slumped. "Lots of planes? So what! You could be talking about any airport in the world," he said.

Fox stared at Zac.

"Do you have absolutely no idea what the Great Icy Pole's like?" Fox blurted out.

Zac shrugged.

"It's the remotest, least explored place on earth," Fox said. "It gets down to minus 40 degrees there in winter. If you so much as go outside without the right gear on, your eyes will freeze solid in their sockets and your fingers will snap off!"

Now Fox had Zac's attention. Maybe this Great Icy Pole place would be kind of cool after all.

"Two, maybe three, boats per summer go to the Pole," said Fox. "They deliver food to the scientists who live at the research station there. But in the last few weeks there's been a couple of planes a day, as well as lots of boats."

Zac had to admit it did sound suspicious.

"So why's GIB sending me?" asked Zac. "Can't they check out what's going on using WorldEye?"

WorldEye is GIB's whiz-bang satellite. It's so powerful it can read a newspaper headline from 500 miles up. Normally, WorldEye is invaluable for surveillance work.

"The Great Icy Pole is so remote, it's

out of satellite range. There's no coverage down there," Fox explained.

"Does that mean—" Zac began.

"Yes, I'm afraid so. Your SpyPad won't work down there. You'll be completely unreachable."

No relying on his satellite GPS navigation software for directions! No calling Leon for help with technical questions! No clues from Mission Control during the mission!

This was going to be tough.

"Since you'll be out of contact, we need

to arrange a pickup time once your fact-finding mission's complete. A GIB transport team will be back to get you exactly 24 hours from the time I picked you up. That's 2:05 p.m. tomorrow."

"What if we miss each other?" asked Zac.

"That can't happen," said Fox sternly. "For safety reasons, air traffic is only allowed around the Great Icy Pole during the summer. It's almost winter down there now. The cutoff date for air traffic is tomorrow."

"So, if I don't catch the helicopter tomorrow—"

"You'll be frozen in down there for months," Fox said, butting in. "You'll have no food and no way to let us know where you are."

"Right," said Zac. "I'd better be ready then, I guess."

Zac stared out the window, thinking about the mission ahead. Then he noticed a cruise ship sailing in the sea below. And closing in fast behind it was another, much smaller, ship.

Fox looked over Zac's shoulder at the two ships below.

"The big one's a luxury cruise ship," Fox explained. "Rich Americans seal spotting and looking at the icebergs."

"And the smaller ship?"

"Pirates, probably," said Fox.

"Pirates!" said Zac, disbelieving.

Pirates wore eye patches and flew the skull and crossbones. Pirates belonged in children's storybooks, not in real life.

"I know it's hard to believe, but there are modern day pirates in this area. They storm aboard tourist ships and steal watches, jewelery, and cash. Sometimes tourists get even get killed," said Fox.

"There must be something we can do!" said Zac.

"This area's so remote, it's pretty much impossible to enforce the law," Fox said.

Zac stood up.

"What are you doing?" asked Fox, looking alarmed.

"I just had an idea," said Zac.

CHAPTER... ...THREE

Before Fox could stop him, Zac had pulled on a jumpsuit and strapped on his parachute gear. Then, Zac strapped a wakeboard to his feet and tied the towrope firmly to the helicopter's door handle.

"Zac! What about the mission?" said Fox, getting angry.

Zac checked his watch.

It was still only 6:43 p.m.

What was Fox talking about? He had plenty of time to complete the mission before the team came to pick him up!

"It's not safe!" said Fox, sounding a lot like Zac's mom.

But Zac wasn't listening. Whether it was good or bad for the mission, Zac couldn't just watch pirates terrorize innocent people.

Zac opened the helicopter door. A gust of cold sea air blew in. Zac took a deep breath.

And then he jumped.

Freefall! No matter how many times Zac jumped from planes and helicopters, his heart always ended up in his mouth.

A few seconds later, Zac pulled his rip cord and his chute opened.

Relief!

But Zac knew skydiving was the easy part. Tackling the gang of pirates would be much tougher!

With a big splash, Zac's wakeboard hit the water. The helicopter hovered high overhead, dragging him along behind it.

Zac signaled to the helicopter to move closer to the pirate ship. Fox understood him and flew the helicopter closer and closer to the ship.

One of Zac's rules for living was:

ZAC'S RULE FOR LIVING - NUMBER 16
NEVER GO ANYWHERE WITHOUT MUSIC TO LISTEN TO.

G·I·B

So even though he was in the middle of the sea, speeding toward a pirate ship, Zac had packed his iPod.

He held onto the towrope with one hand. With the other, he pulled his iPod out of his pocket. He scrolled through his music collection.

Yes . . . there it was! *Maria Vendetta Sings Italian Opera Classics.*

Zac kept a couple of really embarrassing tracks on his iPod in case they ever came in handy on missions. Like today!

In his other pocket, Zac had Leon's latest and coolest invention—Assault Speakers. Loud enough to pierce the eardrums of anyone they're aimed at, according to Leon.

Even at a normal volume, Maria Vendetta has a piercing voice. Zac thought she sounded like a cat whose tail had been stepped on, a million times in a row.

The Assault Speakers come with a pair of soft earplugs to protect the ears of the operator. Zac squashed them into his ears. Then he hit play on his iPod.

Zac turned up the volume on the Assault Speakers. He aimed them at the pirate ship.

"Eeeeeeeeeeeeee!" sang Maria.

Zac's eyes watered. The Assault Speakers vibrated.

And then Zac turned the volume up one more notch!

"OH, MAMMA MIIIIIIIIIIIIIIIIIIIIIIIIIA!" Maria screeched.

The sound was unbearable!

Zac grabbed his SpyPad and popped up the built-in telescope. On the deck of the pirate ship, a collection of rough looking men were fighting over who would be lucky enough to escape belowdecks first. Every single one of the pirates had his fingers jammed in his ears.

"MAMMA MIIIIIIIIIIIA"

Obviously the pirates felt the same way about Maria Vendetta as Zac did.

Up ahead, the tourist boat was gunning

its engines. It sped away from the pirate ship as fast as it could. The decks were lined with wrinkly men and white-haired women dripping with diamonds. Zac waved up at them. They clapped and cheered. They were saved!

Zac knew he'd done the right thing, jumping from the helicopter and stopping the pirates. But as Fox hauled him up by the towrope, Zac couldn't help taking a good, long minute to think about the mission ahead.

Zac's spying missions had taken him to some far-off places. And he'd certainly conquered some tough enemies. But somehow, the Great Icy Pole felt different.

It was lonely.

It was lawless.

It was dangerous and bitterly cold.

It felt like anything could happen to you out here. And if it did, no one would ever find you.

Zac was now an experienced solo spy. But for the first time in his spying career, he was going to be alone on this mission.

Really and truly alone.

CHAPTER... ...FOUR

Zac's pirate-frightening side mission had eaten up a lot of time. It was 9:12 p.m. already!

They were almost at the Great Icy Pole. Fox had to cram Zac's cold weather survival instructions into half the time he'd planned.

"Here's your snowsuit and thermal underwear. Also your hat, goggles, and gloves," said Fox.

Zac nodded. Pretty standard stuff.

"And this is . . . well. It's a little bit special," said Fox, holding up what looked like an oversized doggy pooper-scooper.

"The Great Icy Pole is one of the world's last true wilderness regions," Fox continued. "Naturally, there's no plumbing down there. And the ground is frozen solid. So when you do your business, you just . . ."

Fox snapped the pooper-scooper open and closed.

" . . . take it with you!" he finished, blushing a violent red.

"I think I'm going to be sick," said Zac.

This was a long, long way from being cool.

"Look! Here's where we're going to land," said Fox, glad to have finished the bathroom conversation.

The helicopter touched down behind a towering wall of ice. Even in the gathering gloom of night, the glacier shimmered like sugar. Beyond the glacier, a plain of solid ice stretched right out to the horizon.

Wind howled across the ice. A gang of penguins huddled together for warmth, beaks tucked into their chests.

"This is a covert operation, Zac. There's a group of scientists based at the seal research station over there. . . ."

Fox pointed. Zac could just make out an igloo-shaped building way across the ice.

"We believe they are harmless enough. Still, you mustn't let them know you're here. The idea is to watch for suspicious activity without anyone knowing they're being observed."

Zac nodded. He jumped from the helicopter.

"And remember. Meet the pickup team back here tomorrow or you're a goner," called Fox, waving a cheerful good-bye.

Then, in a flurry of snow and icy wind, the helicopter was gone.

Zac switched on his flashlight and looked around. It was the same blank whiteness in every direction. Even an experienced spy like Zac could easily lose himself in a place like this. He took out his compass.

Zac wasn't used to using such old-fashioned equipment. But he had no Spy-Pad with GPS to rely on here.

Zac paced slowly forward. Icy wind blasted him backward. It was hard going.

For hours, Zac searched for something—anything!—out of the ordinary. But apart from the seal research station, the entire Great Icy Pole seemed deserted.

Zac started feeling annoyed. *Is it possible GIB is wrong about the so-called suspicious activity going on down here?*

There was absolutely nothing to see except a lone seal flapping slowly along the ice.

A seal! *How cute,* as his mom would say.

Zac bent down for a closer look. There was something funny about the seal. Something about its left flipper didn't look quite right.

The seal flopped onto its side. It must be injured! Zac wondered if there was anything he could do. He didn't know much about seals. But he couldn't just leave behind an animal sick and in pain.

The seal seemed to be going from bad to worse. Now there was smoke pouring from its ears.

Hmm, thought Zac. *I'm no expert, but that doesn't look normal.*

Zac reached out and touched the seal. Instead of being warm and soft, the seal felt hard and cold as metal. Then

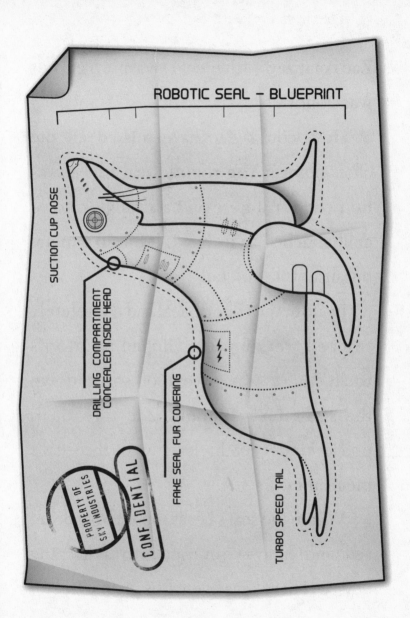

ROBOTIC SEAL — BLUEPRINT

SUCTION CUP NOSE

DRILLING COMPARTMENT
CONCEALED INSIDE HEAD

FAKE SEAL FUR COVERING

TURBO SPEED TAIL

PROPERTY OF
SKY INDUSTRIES

CONFIDENTIAL

Zac realized—the seal wasn't real. It was robotic!

How could Zac have missed all the clues before? The robotic seal had a suction cup for a nose and a strange kind of drill attached to its head. It felt like metal because it *was* metal!

By now, the robotic seal had completely stopped working. Zac flipped it onto its back. There was a row of snaps down the seal's furry tummy. Zac tore them open. Underneath, he found the seal's mechanics.

Where the seal's heart should have been, red and blue wires ran into a homing device. There was even a built-in clock.

Time was slipping away fast!

If Zac could rewire the seal, maybe it would quickly lead him to the suspicious activity he was looking for! A robotic seal seemed like a sure sign that something funny *really was* going on.

Zac unzipped a pocket on the arm of his snowsuit. He'd stashed a miniature tool kit there, just in case. It was almost impossible to use such tiny tools with his thick gloves on.

But he couldn't take his gloves off! Fox said he'd risk frostbite if he did. A frostbitten hand would turn black and eventually fall off, dead.

That was about the grossest thing Zac could think of. He kept his gloves on as he tinkered away.

There, thought Zac, attaching one last blue wire to a red one. He turned the seal on. Instantly, it clapped its flippers and meowed like a cat.

Zac switched off the seal.

That can't be right!

Zac fiddled with a few more wires.

How about that?

He turned the seal back on. This time it moved its flippers perfectly. Only trouble was, the seal kept making big, loud burps.

One last time, Zac fiddled with the wires. He tried the seal again. That was it! The seal was working, all right.

In fact, it was taking off at top speed across the ice!

CHAPTER... ...FIVE

WHOOSH! WHIRR!

The robotic seal sped away. Zac raced after it across the ice. But running was impossible! Zac slipped. He slid. He fell flat on his butt a hundred times.

Where is the seal heading? Toward the seal research station, it looked like.

Does that mean the researchers are up to no good, after all? wondered Zac.

By this time, he was panting hard. The GIB training manual said that a spy must be in peak physical condition at all times. And Zac was. But still, he was no match for a machine. He was exhausted.

They neared the research station. Outside was a row of gleaming new snowmobiles. There was no one around. The first snowmobile even had keys dangling from the ignition. Obviously the seal researchers weren't expecting company.

I'll have it back before they even know I've taken it, thought Zac. And just to make sure . . .

A box of firewood stood beside the snowmobiles. With all his might, Zac dragged the heavy box in front of the research station door. The researchers would be locked in, at least for a while.

Zac didn't know whether they were good or evil yet. But he wasn't taking any chances.

Zac jumped onto the snowmobile.

Twisting back the handlebars, he revved the engine. Then he took off. He sped toward a huge pile of snow and jumped it.

He flew through the air. Awesome!

By now, the robotic seal had left the research station way behind. It seemed to be heading even deeper into the icy wilderness. The homing device inside the seal was obviously very powerful. The seal was heading, straight as an arrow, for somewhere in particular.

But where?

Zac accelerated. He practically flew across the ice toward the seal. He was going to find out!

Then Zac saw a shape looming up out

of the gloom. Ahead there were some huge, round storage tanks. Beside those were some long sheds.

It must be some kind of top secret storage facility, thought Zac.

Zac felt sure he was getting closer to cracking the mission. Good thing, too. It was already 5:53 a.m.

The GIB team would be there to collect him in eight hours.

Zac parked close to one of the storage tanks, where the snowmobile would be in the shadows. He cut the snowmobile's engine. The sun would be up soon, and Zac couldn't be sure who was watching.

With ice crunching loudly under his snow boots, Zac followed the robotic seal on foot. Silently, the seal slithered over to one of the storage tanks.

Zac watched carefully. The storage tank was fitted with a valve, right down at ground level. Using the suction cup on its nose, the robotic seal anchored itself to the tank. Then, a hose popped up from underneath a hatch in the seal's back. The hose connected to the valve perfectly.

Instantly, the air was filled with a very strong smell. It was a smell Zac recognized. *But what is it?* Zac sniffed again.

It's gasoline!

Zac raced over to the storage tank. A metal ladder was attached to the side. Zac climbed up. On the roof of the storage tank, Zac found a window. He turned on his flashlight and shined it through the glass.

The tank was full of gasoline!

Pieces of the puzzle began to come together in Zac's mind. The gas shortage his dad had mentioned. Those tankers mysteriously sinking. Suspicious activity at the Great Icy Pole. And, even more fishy, robotic seals with drills and suction cups!

Zac's sharp spying brain turned the

pieces around and around until he had a theory that made sense.

Robotic seals were drilling into tankers out at sea and stealing gasoline. That explained the global gas shortage.

If you have tankers with tiny seal holes drilled in the side, this would explain why the tankers kept sinking.

The suspicious activity at the Great Icy Pole must somehow be linked to the weird gasoline storage facility.

But even as Zac thought this through, more questions occurred to him. *Who is stealing the gas? And, more to the point, why?*

Zac wished he could use his SpyPad. Then he could discuss his suspicions with

GIB. Mission Control would have some ideas. But being out of satellite range meant he would just have to figure it out on his own!

Just then, Zac wished even harder that he could call Mission Control for help. Because zooming toward him at top speed, were a bunch of thugs on snowmobiles!

CHAPTER SIX

His heart pounding, Zac raced to find somewhere to hide. The thugs on snow-mobiles were shouting and waving angrily. They didn't look too happy to discover they weren't alone in the Great Icy Pole.

Are they from the seal research station? They have to be!

The snowmobiles roared toward Zac. Closer. Closer!

Luckily, Zac spotted the perfect hiding place. A big wooden crate stamped with the words, "extra seal flippers." Just in the nick of time, Zac ducked down behind it, out of sight.

"Whoever locked us in has got to be around here somewhere," an angry voice growled.

"Yeah, I bet it's probably GIB," replied a woman. "I hate those GIB goody-goodies."

Goody-goodies? Maybe Leon, but not me! thought Zac.

"Hey!" said the woman. "Footsteps!"

Oh, no!

"I'll just follow them until I find where . . . aha!" said the woman.

With an iron grip, a gloved hand grabbed Zac's shoulders.

"Look who we have here. A GIB spy. Zac Power, if I'm not mistaken," said the woman.

How does she know my name? Zac wondered. *This gang must really know their stuff!*

Zac's eyes slid across to the woman's expensive looking wristwatch.

He just didn't have time to get captured right now!

Suddenly, Zac twisted free of the woman's grip. As fast as he could, he ran toward the snowmobile he'd hidden in the shadows. He could hear heavy footsteps behind him.

"Leaving so soon?" asked the man, sounding angry. In a second, he'd caught up to Zac.

"You should lie down," the man said.

Lie down? Why? Zac wondered.

Then . . .

CRRRRRRUNCH!

The man punched Zac in the nose!

"You shouldn't run around when you've got a broken nose, Zac," he went on, smugly.

Pain. Zac's whole face pulsed with it. Grey spots floated before his eyes.

Zac bent over double. His nose was seriously hurting. Blood trickled from his nose and splashed on the snow.

Snow . . .

That was it!

Still bent over and groaning with pain for effect, Zac was sure the thugs didn't know what he was doing.

Standing up, he chucked the snowballs he'd made right in their faces.

THWACK!

THWACK!

THWACK!

All right! Three direct hits.

Without looking back, Zac ran for the snowmobile. But blood was still streaming from his nose. If he didn't stop it, the splashes of red on the snow were going to show the gang exactly which way he'd gone.

Zac fished around in his backpack for a tissue. His mom had given him some.

Zac held the tissue up to his aching nose.

Whoa . . . what a weird feeling, thought Zac.

The sky went blurry. The snow seemed to swim. He was so sleepy all of a sudden. . . .

Too late, Zac realized what he had done. He'd used one of his mom's Total Knockout Tissues, the ones that put you to sleep as soon as you hold them near your nose. They were supposed to be for enemies!

I'm really in trouble . . . I've got to . . . thought Zac, his eyelids drooping.

Before he could finish that thought, Zac was fast asleep!

CHAPTER... ...SEVEN

Zac opened his eyes sleepily. He yawned loudly and scratched his head all over.

Just another day with nothing much to do, Zac thought. *Might have a bowl of Chocmallow Puffs for breakfast, play a little guitar . . .*

Zac looked around. He didn't seem to be in his bed.

That's strange . . . And . . . oh, no! Where are my pj's?

Instead of being safe at home in his bedroom, Zac was in some kind of laboratory. Somehow, he seemed to be hovering in midair. And he was wearing nothing but a pair of metal underpants!

Then Zac remembered what had happened. He'd accidentally knocked himself out with his mom's Total Knockout Tissues. The evil researchers must have brought him back to the seal research station and locked him up.

He checked his watch.

It was already 12:09 p.m.

He'd been out cold so long, there were only two hours left to crack the mission in time to make his ride home.

But, just then, Zac had other problems to solve. Such as, how on earth was he hovering in midair? And what was going on with these metal underpants?

Zac looked up. On the ceiling, directly above him, Zac saw a giant magnet. He looked down. Sure enough, underneath him was another giant magnet. Zac wriggled one way, then the other. But he couldn't move!

It was strange. There wasn't anything visible holding him in place. And yet Zac couldn't move an inch!

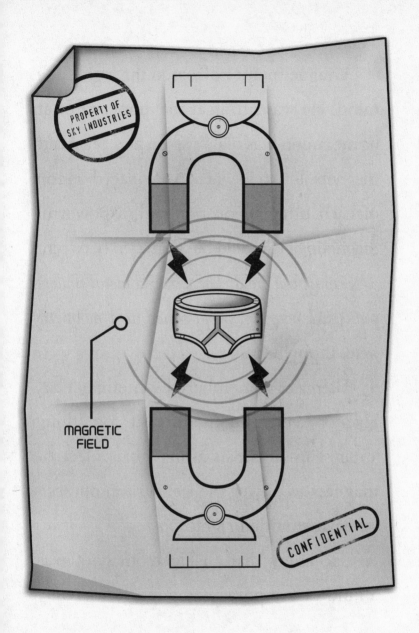

PROPERTY OF
SKY INDUSTRIES

MAGNETIC
FIELD

CONFIDENTIAL

A vague memory floated through Zac's mind. He was sitting at the dinner table at home. Leon was blabbing on and on about magnets. If two magnets were placed on top of each other, Leon had said, a powerful magnetic field would be created in between.

A magnetic field! These stupid metal underpants are keeping me prisoner in a magnetic field, thought Zac.

Then Zac remembered something else. Hadn't Leon also mentioned something about top scientists using giant electromagnets to power their supercomputers? That sounded right. . . .

Zac knew that an electromagnet was a kind of temporary magnet. It was only magnetic when an electrical current was running through it.

I'm in a research station where there are plenty of computers, so it makes sense that this is an electromagnet I'm trapped in, reasoned Zac to himself. *So if I can turn off the power supply, the magnets will demagnetize and I'll be free!*

But turning off the power supply to a sophisticated electromagnet wasn't going to be easy, not when Zac was trapped in midair wearing nothing but a pair of metal undies!

Desperately, Zac looked around. If only he could spot exactly where the electro-magnet was plugged in.

Over in the corner of the room, Zac spotted a power strip with seven or eight things plugged into it. *The electromagnet is plugged in there, too—it has to be!*

An idea popped into Zac's head. It was a little gross. But what was that phrase Zac's granny sometimes used?

DESPERATE TIMES CALL FOR GROSS MEASURES!
– ZAC'S GRANNY (AGENT WRINKLES) –
G·I·B

Or something like that.

Zac concentrated hard. He thought of pizza—his favorite was Mexicana, with spicy beef, sour cream, and corn chips on top.

Immediately, spit jetted into his mouth and pooled in his cheeks.

His plan was working!

Next, Zac thought of chocolate ice cream sundaes with cookie dough pieces and hot chocolate sauce. Even more spit rushed into his mouth.

I'm ready, thought Zac.

He gathered all his spit into one, huge mouthful. Then, with all the power he had in his cheeks, he hocked the world's biggest-ever spit glob in the direction of the power strip.

SSSSSSPLAT!

With a loud, wet noise, the spit glob landed on the power strip.

FIZZ! SPLUTTER!

There was a shower of blue sparks. The computers stopped humming. The room went dark. Zac had short-circuited the power.

And suddenly, Zac was falling. He hit the ground with a loud clang of metal underpants. But it didn't matter.

He was free!

CHAPTER ...EIGHT

With the power off, it was pitch black in the research station.

Lucky for me! thought Zac. He still had no clothes on except for the metal underpants. He would have died if anyone had seen him like that!

Moving fast, Zac headed for the door. To crack this mission, he still had to find out why the evil researchers were stealing the gas. And he had to find out quickly!

Just over an hour until his flight home.

Zac peered through the glass panel set into the door. Outside, he saw a long corridor. Directly across the hall was a big laboratory packed with fancy equipment.

Could it be the command center of the entire evil operation?

Scientists and researchers streamed out of the lab. Zac recognized some of them as the thugs he'd encountered at the storage facility. But there were plenty of others, too. This was no small operation!

"Power must be restored! We're so close now! We can't afford to lose a minute!" one of the researchers was yelling. People scattered all over the building, trying to find out where the short circuit had happened. Pretty soon, the main lab was totally empty.

Clanking awkwardly, Zac made his way into the corridor and into the main lab. And there, on the very first bench, was a pile of clothes. They were his! Checking first that he was alone, Zac whipped off the metal undies and put his own clothes back on. Relief!

Coolness restored, Zac felt ready to search the lab from top to bottom. Then, overhead, there was a flickering. The lights came back on. That must mean the computers were working again. The researchers would be back any minute!

Zac didn't have much time.

He rushed over to a computer in the very middle of the room. It was labeled, "server."

It looked like the main computer—hopefully the one that stored all the information Zac needed to find out what these people were up to.

Zac tapped a few keys. But all that

happened was the computer's screen saver changed from flowers to a photo of a kitten. This was no good! How was he supposed to get into the actual files?

This was where Zac needed Leon's help. But instead he'd have to call on his inner geek and figure it out for himself!

Then Zac remembered something. Hadn't that researcher yelled out that they were close now?

Maybe the last document opened on the computer will hold the key.

Grabbing the mouse, Zac went to the File menu and selected Recent Documents. The most recent document on the list was called Operation WorldEye.doc.

WorldEye! thought Zac, surprised. *GIB's incredibly high tech satellite system? What does that have to do with the stolen gasoline?*

Zac opened the document.

He scanned what was written there.

MEMO
TO ALL SKY INDUSTRIES STAFF

OPERATION WORLDEYE – DAILY UPDATE

Gasoline storage tanks are
at 98.97% storage capacity.
This is almost enough fuel
to fire our ballistic missile.
We anticipate total destruction of the
WorldEye satellite system within hours.
Great work, team!

P.S. DON'T FORGET, we're collecting money
to buy milk and coffee for the staff room.
Have you contributed yet?

It all seemed horribly clear, except for two things. Who was Sky Industries and why would they want to blow up World-Eye?

The walls of the lab were lined with photographs of important Sky Industries staff shaking hands with dignitaries.

Zac recognized the Prime Minister of Japan, some American senators, and . . . wasn't that . . . yes, it was! The Commander-in-Chief of GIB!

The Commander-in-Chief was standing with a group of men and women dressed in Sky Industries lab coats. Behind them was a large piece of equipment. Zac could just make out some words painted on the side—WorldEye.

WorldEye! So, Sky Industries manufactured WorldEye? Why on earth would they want to blow it up if they made it?

Unless . . .

Zac thought about the companywide e-mail. Sky Industries was collecting money from staff to buy cheap things like milk and coffee!

If the company can't even afford those, the business can't be going very well, thought Zac.

Zac knew that WorldEye was the most expensive satellite ever built. *Could Sky Industries want to blow it up just so they can get the contract to build a replacement? That way, they'd get their business out of financial trouble. That's it! It has to be.*

The gasoline storage tanks were almost full. The missile launch couldn't be far away. Zac would have to do something right now to stop it. Otherwise, it would be too late!

CHAPTER... ...NINE

"OK, then. Back to work."

Zac's blood ran cold. That voice! He recognized it! It was the woman with the iron grip who'd discovered him back at the storage facility. And, by the sound of things, she had all her coworkers from the lab with her.

He really didn't want another encounter with that woman. She was as tough as nails.

The handle on the lab door turned. In another second, Zac would be caught.

Apart from the door, there was only one other way out. Without a moment's hesitation, Zac vaulted onto the nearest lab bench. Then, nimble as a monkey, he jumped up and swung from the ceiling fan across to a window high up in the wall.

With less than half an inch to spare, Zac caught the window ledge. He swung by his fingertips for a second.

The lab door creaked open just as Zac, with a huge effort, hauled himself up and out through the window. Just in time.

THUNK! *OWWWW!*

Outside, he hit the ice heavily.

There was no time to worry about cuts and bruises, though. Zac got up and ran. Just as before, a line of snowmobiles stood ready and waiting to be used by the researchers.

Or by 12-year-old superspies, thought Zac.

Jumping on a snowmobile, Zac revved the accelerator. Time check!

He had to stop the missile launch and get his helicopter ride home, all by 2:05 p.m.!

Zac roared off in the direction of the storage facility. Wind howled around him. It was snowing hard.

Zac could hardly see two feet in front of him, so it was a minute or two before he noticed.

He was totally surrounded by robotic seals! Waves and waves of seals were moving across the ice toward the storage facility. With so many seals full of stolen gas, there'd soon be more than enough gas to launch the missile.

I can stop the missile launch, thought Zac, *if I can stop these seals from reaching the storage facility.*

But there were hundreds—maybe even thousands—of robotic seals! How could he possibly stop them all in the next few minutes?

Unless . . .

The robotic seals are full of gas. Gasoline is highly flammable. So . . .

The plan seemed too good to be true. Zac could hardly believe he was going to get to do something so cool, and all in the name of saving the world!

LASER BEAM
>>> ON

LASER OPTION
>>> RED HOT

Zac dug in his pocket and pulled out his Spy-Pad. It hadn't been very useful on this mission so far. But now it would be. The SpyPad's powerful built-in laser was going to come in very handy!

Zac aimed the laser at the nearest seal, scooting along behind it on his snowmobile.

At first, nothing happened.

But slowly, very slowly, the robotic seal's artificial fur began to smoke.

As Zac watched, the fake fur caught fire.

Then, flames took over. The robotic seal was swallowed up, and . . .

KERRRRRRRRR - BANG!

Enormous fireball!

Smoke! Scorching heat!

The seal exploded, sending a shower of flaming robot parts all over the ice.

BANG! BANG! BANG!

The flaming robot parts set other seals on fire, and they exploded, too. Zac had managed to get rid of all the seals and their precious cargo of gasoline . . . all in one go. It was pretty cool to watch, even if Zac did say so himself.

But Zac didn't have an extra second to stand around and gloat. He had a helicopter flight to catch!

CHAPTER ...TEN

Zac roared off on the snowmobile. Where exactly was he supposed to meet the pickup team again? He thought he remembered.

As Zac scanned the horizon for the meeting point, a terrible thought crept into his mind. Yes, he'd blown up the seals and their gasoline supplies. Sure, he'd saved WorldEye *for now*. But what if he hadn't saved it permanently?

Even though Zac had destroyed this batch of gasoline, Sky Industries could just start collecting gas all over again. They still only needed a small amount to bring their storage tanks up to 100% capacity!

Zac thought about Sky Industries and what kind of people worked there. They'd gone to all the trouble of inventing robotic seals just to steal gas. They'd probably stop at nothing to steal a tiny bit more. After all, they'd be iced in all winter at the Great Icy Pole. That would give them time to get up to all sorts of tricks!

If I truly want to save WorldEye, I've got to destroy the actual missile, thought Zac grimly.

He checked his watch.

His flight home was due to leave in nine minutes! And it was his only chance to get home before all flights to the Great Icy Pole would be shut down for the winter.

If he missed the flight, he'd be stuck in this icy wilderness with a bunch of very angry people from Sky Industries for months and months.

But Zac knew if he didn't destroy the missile before he left the Great Icy Pole, WorldEye would be in serious danger over the months to come.

It was an impossible decision!

There must be something he was missing, some other way to solve the problem.

Zac's mind spun into overdrive. He had an idea. It was risky. But so were his other options. Trusting his spy instincts as always, Zac made a quick decision. He was going to go for it. After all, it wasn't a Zac Power mission without a little risk!

Zac turned the snowmobile around. Instead of heading for the meeting point, he went back in the direction of the storage facility. Zac remembered seeing a large silo beside the storage tanks and all the sheds.

That must be where they're keeping the missile! thought Zac.

He sped toward the silo.

He checked his watch.

He'd totally missed his flight by now. *This plan had better work,* said Zac to himself, as a kind of nervous excitement bubbled up in his stomach. It was one of Zac's all-time favorite feelings.

Zac pulled up at the silo. Wasting no time, he marched over to the security door. It was bolted shut, of course. Using his patented combination of a credit card, a coat hanger, spit, and a ball of string, Zac picked the lock.

Lucky he'd paid so much attention in

that Covert Lockpicking class back in his Spy Training days.

The door sprang open. A giant missile, twice the size of Zac, stood in the very center of the silo.

Zac rummaged in his backpack for his tool kit. This next part of the plan was going to involve some craftsmanship. Zac had often seen Leon weld bits and pieces together while he was experimenting with new gadgets.

But Leon had never tried welding the driver's seat and controls from a snowmobile onto a ballistic missile before!

Zac set to work. Using the laser from his SpyPad, Zac cut the seat off of the snowmobile. Then, with welding gear from his tool kit, he attached the seat and its glass cover to the side of the missile.

Zac even surprised himself. In less than an hour, the job was finished.

Zac was very pleased. This time, he'd really saved WorldEye—he was going to take the missile with him.

There were only three more things left to do. Find the ignition button, jump into the driver's seat, and hang on tight!

The button glowed green in the darkness. Zac took a deep breath. Then, before he could change his mind about the plan (surely his most far-out yet!), he slammed his hand down on the button.

The countdown had begun!

...10
...9
...8

Zac leapt into the driver's seat.

...7
...6
...5

He yanked down the glass bubble protecting the driver's seat.

...4
...3
...2
...1

He braced himself.

BLASTOFF!

At the very last second, the roof of the silo slid away. Zac shot through the hole in the top and into the icy sky outside.

This was more than flying!

This was . . . well . . . rocketing!

Zac streaked across the sky. At this rate, he'd be back at the Power family beach house in time for the second day of summer vacation.

As he got closer to the beach house, Zac's SpyPad suddenly beeped. It was back in range.

MESSAGE RECEIVED
2:59 PM

Once your
mission's complete,
hurry back home.
We're having burgers and
fries on the beach and
yours are getting cold.

MESSAGE FROM
AGENT TLC (MOM)

VACATION MODE
>>> ON

Cool! Burgers and fries on the beach.

His mom didn't need to worry about them getting cold.

He'd be home soon.

Say, about 47 seconds from now!